I0566502

Sherlock Holmes and The Affair of The Contentious Contralto

by
Fiona Jane Brown

© Copyright 2014
Fiona-Jane Brown

The right of Fiona-Jane Brown to be identified as the authors of this work has been asserted by her in accordance with the Copyright, Designs and Patents Act 1988.

All rights reserved. No reproduction, copy or transmission of this publication may be made without express prior written permission. No paragraph of this publication may be reproduced, copied or transmitted except with express prior written permission or in accordance with the provisions of the Copyright Act 1956 (as amended). Any person who commits any unauthorised act in relation to this publication may be liable to criminal prosecution and civil claims for damage.

All characters appearing in this work are fictitious. Any resemblance to real persons, living or dead, is purely coincidental. The opinions expressed herein are those of the authors and not of MX Publishing.

Paperback ISBN 9781780926124
ePub ISBN 9781780926131
PDF ISBN 9781780926148

Published in the UK by MX Publishing
335 Princess Park Manor, Royal Drive,
London, N11 3GX – United Kingdom
www.mpublishing.co.uk

Cover design by www.staunch.com

To my very talented friends Jonathan Goodwin, Gary Archer, Ross K Foad and Mike Archer who inspired me afresh with their portrayals of the traditional Holmes and Watson.

If it ain't broke, don't fix it!

It was with some trepidation I had returned to live at 221b Baker Street with my old friend, Sherlock Holmes in the summer of 1910. London in the new century seemed as ripe a harvest as ever for my friend's now world-renowned deductive powers. Our new king, His Royal Highness, George V, had recourse to employ Holmes in a delicate matter on the Sandringham Estate, doubtless involving a priceless reward, the details of which my friend would never divulge. Yet I soon found that we fell into each other's little ways again; Holmes' untidiness, his often malodorous chemical experiments, and of course, the one thing that often gave me joy, his violin playing. At peace, Holmes could produce the most exquisite melodies, to a standard matching that of his musical heroine, Madame Neruda, who had become the royal violinist but nine years past. Thus, the widower and the bachelor jostled along together as though it was still the 1880s.

We are no longer young men — indeed, Holmes has developed a rather theatrical white streak through his once jet black locks and I have since given up all attempt to tame a now wiry head of thinning hair. Yet my friend's alternating periods of vigour and languor have not varied one iota. I have work enough in my general practice, and am occasionally called upon to give lectures at the Medical Society attached to St Bartholomew's Hospital. The students are always keen to offer their services in assisting with house-calls, as had been the case one rather damp August evening at a particularly difficult delivery in St. John's Wood. After much travail, and ultimately, the use of forceps and some chloroform to ease her pain, the mother was deliriously happy to be delivered of a new son, a much-wished for child, she already being mother to four daughters. I thanked my student, sending him home to his digs in a cab at my expense and decided to take a slow stroll through Regent's Park to ease the journey homeward.

It was ten o'clock in the morning when I wearily climbed the stairs at Baker Street, being greeted by our stalwart housekeeper, Mrs Hudson. She is now aided in providing for our comfort by her daughter and a pageboy, ironically called Billy, as was the name of our first young messenger all those years ago. Mrs Hudson saw my fatigued expression and offered breakfast, but I begged of her only a cup of warm milk as I was intending to go straight to bed for a few hours, knowing I could rely on my practice partner, a promising young medic from Edinburgh, to attend to morning surgery.

I entered the drawing room, my eyes hardly able to remain open, dropped my bag by the armchair, but just as I was about to sink into its finely upholstered embrace, I became acutely aware of Holmes' presence. He sat in this chair, partly dressed in that tattered Paisley housecoat he insists on keeping, his shirt, waistcoat, trousers, and socked feet in a pair of leather slippers with which Mrs Hudson's daughter had presented him for his birthday. His expression was one of intense glee. I was sure he wished to tantalise me with that aquiline gaze until I was forced to enquire into the nature of his obvious pleasure, yet

I quickly struggled out of my jacket, too exhausted to play his little game.

"Ah, Watson! Mother and baby well?" Holmes trilled.

"Dash it, Holmes, how on earth did you know it was a birth I was attending? I suppose Billy told you!" I replied, unable to comprehend his ever-surprising foreknowledge.

"On the contrary, my dear Watson, I have just arisen from a pleasant slumber not half an hour ago and neither have I seen our young page today nor has Mrs Hudson mentioned it, as she would not have known you left in the early hours of the morning. No, I simply observed and deduced as always, and now, as you remove your jacket I can see my deduction is confirmed by the evidence!" he beamed, turning a cut piece of newsprint in his slender fingers.

Exhausted, I attempted to entertain his almost childlike desire to demonstrate his skills, "Very well, do explain to me what always seems like some sort of necromancy!"

"Believe me, Watson, there is nothing magical or arcane about my method, as you should know very well by now! You came in, looking extremely tired, your eyes being bleary as one would expect from a man who has been up most of the night; secondly, on observing your jacket, I could see your wrists were bare and deduced that you had rolled up your sleeves to carry out some rather messy procedure. Also, there is a faint smear of blood on the back of your right hand, even though your palms are scrubbed clean. This would all lead me to believe you have been in attendance at a rather prolonged labour and that you are so relieved to have delivered the child you have not even unrolled your sleeves after washing your hands for perhaps the umpteenth time. Very simple, eh, my old friend?" Holmes explained. He was as ever, perfectly correct, I realised, as I caught sight of the red stain on my hand.

Draping my jacket on the back of the armchair and unravelling my shirt sleeves, I sighed, "Hum, yes, it is as plain as a pikestaff when you lay it out like that." The smile that played upon his lips still led me to believe he was keen to reveal the contents of the article in his hands, "You are looking unusually pleased with yourself, though, Holmes, I take it something in the morning's post has amused you?"

Like a clever scholar who has been presented with the master's chalk in order to demonstrate a problem on the blackboard, Holmes smiled broadly again, "Oh indeed, Watson, such intriguing correspondence! Here, take a look at this news clipping if you are not too fatigued," he said, reaching across to me as I flumped into the chair.

Retrieving my now much-relied-upon spectacles from my breast pocket and placing them on my nose I began to scan the piece from the society column of the previous night's Evening Standard. ""*Mr and Mrs Godfrey Norton Q.C., of Holland Park, are delighted to announce the engagement of their daughter, Sophie Estella, graduate of the Paris conservatoire and noted concert pianist, to Master James Doyle of Zurich, Switzerland, lately of Fitzwilliam College, Cambridge, reading law; son of retired mountaineer and explorer, Seumas Doyle*", I didn't think you were interested in social gossip, Holmes, why do you smile so at this?" I commented in a puzzled tone.

Holmes pulled another piece of paper, a blush colour, from the mantelpiece where it had been resting under his briarwood pipe. "A capital mistake to theorise before one is in possession of all the evidence, Watson! Now, look at this handbill which represents an invitation from a particular old acquaintance of ours!"

I unfolded the handbill, noticing immediately the heading "*Empire Theatre, Leicester Square*", and to my surprise a very familiar lady's image, "Great heavens! *"Farewell performance of former Prima Donna of the Warsaw Opera and celebrated contralto of New Jersey, USA, Miss Irene Adler, at the Leicester Square Theatre, London*"! Adler! Norton! Of course, Norton was her married name when she… her daughter? Irene Adler has a daughter who is engaged to the son of a mountaineer? And what, you want us to go to her farewell performance? But she was the only woman to … well, to outwit you, Holmes, surely you…" I rubbed my eyes and stared at him, incredulous. He nodded slowly. "… but you do!" I gasped, looking back at the attractive photographic image of Irene Adler, clearly taken a few years ago, but from which her charm fairly oozed. This lady was the only example of the female kind in whom Holmes ever had any interest. He had only referred to her after the affair with the foreign royal as "The Woman" such was his regard for this American singing beauty and adventuress.

"It cannot be too much of a surprise that Miss Adler, now Mrs Norton should have a child, and one of age to be married, it is just over two decades since we last saw her. Indeed she has led an unremarkable life since the business with the King of Bohemia — a man who had far less sense than she! Her husband is the Solicitor-General for all England; no-one could be more respectable! As for my grudging admiration of her, I value the kindness of her invitation to attend the concert, and at last meet face to face the best of all women! The concert is tomorrow night, Watson, and I believe our dinner suits are both clean and ready for use! It is time for a little leisure after so much excitement lately!"

"Ah, you mean your invaluable service to His Majesty? I don't doubt that you earned his eternal gratitude! The case bore a strong resemblance to the *Musgrave Ritual*, would you not agree? I mean, with the vengeful maid and her errant lover? Hmm, for once I am inclined to agree Holmes, and I believe Miss Adler did have a fine reputation for her singing voice," I replied, recalling that earliest of Holmes' adventures which occurred long before I made his acquaintance. I stood up and yawned, "However, I must try and regain some of my lost repose, or I shall be useful for nothing! Young Dr Arthur is a good fellow, but I do not wish to presume too much upon his goodwill, thus I fully intend to carry out my afternoon's appointments, so I will leave you to your musings." I headed back into the corridor to my own room, but before I reached the comfort of that oh-so-attractive bed, I caught Holmes' little soliloquy.

He had retrieved the handbill from my chair and was looking admiringly at Miss Adler, or should I say, Mrs Norton's image. He folded it again and closed his eyes, muttering softly, "Mrs Norton, still the daintiest thing under a bonnet I dare say, if this handbill is anything to go by! And you thought to invite your old sparring partner to your final stage performance? Sweet woman indeed!" he chuckled, rose and swept up the sheaf of papers from the side table which had been at his elbow, and retreated to the sanctuary of his own room. I confess that I remember little after that, having managed into my nightshirt with a struggle and was asleep before I even turned to extinguish the lamp by my bed.

Holland Park is considered to be a grand suburb these days, the abode of eminent bankers, surgeons, and those in the legal profession. One house in particular belongs to the Solicitor-General of England, Godfrey Norton Q.C.; inside the parlour, his wife and daughter are engaged in a battle of words which can only result when mother and child are of the same temperament. Sophie Norton, nineteen years old, but a musical prodigy, having already graduated from the Paris Conservatoire, is forthright and outspoken. Indeed, she is following her mother around the lavish room, pulling at the sleeve of Irene Norton's gown in a furiously insistent manner as her mother wishes only to walk away from her and avoid further conflict.

"But mother! You aren't listening to me! James didn't mean it, he truly didn't, he's just had a little too much, that's all!" Sophie cried.

"Sophie Norton, you have had sufficient education to know the maxim *'in vino veritas'* have you not? Excessive alcohol brings out the true nature of a man; I have seen it on many a Polish back street or New York alleyway! That boy raised his hand to you! The demon of drink obviously betrays his baser character! And to think your father had consented to take him into his law practice! Why did I ever agree to this?" Irene sighed indignantly as she turned to face her daughter.

"Mother!" Sophie began, horrified at what she perceived as her mother's hypocrisy, "You yourself suggested it! I would never have dared to approach Father with such a request! And Father already agreed to the engagement when James asked him! And what's more, this is the twentieth century, the times are coming now when a woman will marry for love not for some mistaken loyalty to old family values!" she continued, folding her arms defensively.

Irene threw her hands in the air, "And fat lot of good a new century has done us, my girl! If it promotes insolence and disrespect in our children and displaces a parent's right to choose a suitable mate for them! And what of your father? If he knew his daughter was going to marry a violent brawler, do you not think he would put a stop to it immediately? I must take this up with him, I cannot allow it to continue when Godfrey has done so much to raise awareness of the plight of ladies trapped in marriages where bruises and broken bones are what they receive for their fidelity!" she retorted.

Sophie dashed forward and grabbed her mother's arm again, "How dare you? How can you compare my James to those men? They are but gutter-trash that treat their wives so, James would never ever knowingly hurt me or any other woman! His grandfather was a high-court judge, he knew about such awful things, and how the sympathy always lay with the drunken layabouts as 'hard-working men' rather than the poor slaves to which their wives were reduced! I love James, I know him by heart, and so I understand that his fondness for alcohol was set in motion by attempting to ape his grander fellows at Cambridge! He dearly wished to be a barrister, and by engaging their friendship, hoped to be brought into the company of their fathers, uncles and even grandfathers who were already in the legal profession! These rich fellows are famous drinkers, like servants of Bacchus, but only in play, they are perfectly capable of being sober law students during term- time! Therefore you cannot compare James to the inhabitants of Kentish town or Southwark! And for that matter, how can you credit me, your own daughter with so little sense? Do you not think I would have broken off our romance if I thought for one moment he would hurt me? How little you must think of me, mother, how very little! I wish you were dead, then I might please myself!" her voice had risen to such a pitch that she had become breathless. She swayed in an ungainly manner, and began to gasp for the service of her maid, "Mary, Mary, where are you? I need my tincture!"

The faithful little servant, a girl with a deep olive complexion, betraying Romany ancestry, came running into the parlour as if she had been waiting by the door, sensing her mistress was in distress. Mary stroked Sophie's back as her mistress coughed violently, "There we are, Miss Sophie, remember what the doctor said, take deep breaths, calm yourself, then take a few sips, this is the diluted solution," she said, in an accent straight from the East End. She produced a little green glass phial from her apron pocket and handed it to Sophie, who composed herself sufficiently to take a brief drink of its contents as Mary supported her.

"Come now, Miss, better you lie down a while," Mary added, steering the wheezing Sophie towards the door.

Irene stood dumbstruck, an expression of terror on her face. A few seconds later, her husband came through the same door, his legal gown flapping behind him. He saw immediately the unnatural paleness in his wife's complexion. The tall, once slender gentleman that Irene had married in favour of her Bohemian admirer, now a sturdy, but contented husband, smiled, "Is something amiss, my dear? You look so upset! Did I just hear raised voices as I came in?" Godfrey said in a gently dismissive tone, as he attempted to defuse the obvious heated atmosphere in the room.

Irene continued to stare at the open door, her eyes having become glassy with tears, such that her husband stepped forward and placed a comforting hand on her shoulder. "I can barely believe it, Godfrey, my own child just wished me dead!" she enunciated, finally recovering her speech.

Godfrey smiled kindly again, knowing his dear girls often fell out of sorts with each other, "Oh come now, a mother and daughter argument? It was in the heat of the moment, dear, she didn't mean it I'm sure. Is young Master Doyle the cause of your little row?"

"Don't make light of it, you did not see the rage in her eyes, the venom in her voice! The girl meant every word, and indeed, her fiancé is at the root of such cruel words!" Irene shrieked, pulling away from him.

Godfrey maintained his composure, as a lifetime in courtrooms had taught him, "Ah, now, evidently he has done something you disapprove of, yet she is defending him to the hilt, hence her emotional outburst, am I right?" he said, holding the lapels of his waistcoat and leaning back a little on his heels.

"Oh Godfrey... I had thought by this time that being a mother would be a joy, not a chore! But yes, the skills which made you a great lawyer prove their worth again! James and Sophie were in the hallway when I entered from here; he was clearly the worse for drink and was stumbling around as Sophie tried to support him. She castigated him lightly and said he was spending too much time with his old Fitzwilliam College friends, whereupon he growled that he wasn't and lifted his hand to strike her. He would have done so had I not yelled at him! He practically crumbled to the ground at the realisation of my presence, foolish boy! I told him to get out of the house immediately, and then Sophie started screaming in his defence. What are we to do? The boy clearly has a problem!" Irene explained sorrowfully, wringing her hands as she did so.

Godfrey frowned, seeing that the argument was slightly more than maternal over-concern. "Hmm, I can see now why it should have caused so much upset. But truly, the boy is of a good family, and having so recently lost his mother, it is not entirely surprising that he should be tempted back into bad habits by his old college chums!" he observed, musing on the exploits of his own fellow students while at university. He patted Irene's shoulder again, "I think it would be best if I talk to him, he should be frightened to face you after such disgraceful conduct. But do not worry about Sophie, she is a sensible girl."

Irene seized her husband's arm, "Oh please be right, my darling, I can't bear the thought that she should end up like my poor aunt Eleanor! She had a husband who was sweet as pie to her when they were first married but slowly she saw how he loved the whisky bottle more than her. Everything she did was wrong! He became a sneak, hurting her where no-one could see! My own mother said she couldn't understand why Eleanor was always struggling with 'back pain' as she called it. You know what happened to her, don't you? What an end for a lady who had been destined to become a talented teacher, if not the headmistress at Sweet Briar College in the Blue Ridge Mountains!" Tears began to streak down Irene's cheeks. Godfrey swept his arms around her and she leaned her head against his shoulder.

"Yes, sadly I do recall. She was found at the bottom of the stairs with a broken neck. Her husband disappeared, but then the neighbours started gossiping, and her post-mortem showed far more injuries than she could have sustained from the fall," he said, remembering Eleanor Fletcher's fate.

"Yes! That rattle snake! He killed her, he battered her all her married life then killed her! I do not want our Sophie to suffer a similar fate!" Irene howled, pulling out of Godfrey's embrace and fleeing the parlour.

"But my dearest, James Doyle is nothing of the kind!" he called after her. He sighed, knowing it best to leave her to weep in peace. "Would that all such men find themselves dangling at the end of a gallows' rope before they do more damage!" he said aloud.

It is a common staying that Time heals many wounds, thus it appeared that the anxiousness and rage Mrs Irene Norton felt towards her daughter the previous evening had all but vanished. We, Holmes and I, had been told when we reached the box office that the lady wished to see us before the performance, and were invited to the green room by theatre manager, Mr Joseph Harrison. He extoled her singing virtues, saying he had been a great admirer of hers from the first time she had ever stood on a London stage. He had been a stagehand in his youth, and had watched, entranced, her first performance as Katisha in *The Mikado*, perhaps not an ideal role for a young woman, but certainly suitable for her vocal range. Mr Harrison explained that Miss Adler would reprise many of her noted pieces at tonight's concert, "*Kastisha's Song*" being one of them.

Harrison knocked on the green room door and entered as we heard a female voice utter "Come in!"

"Miss Adler, your guests are here, two gentlemen, Dr Watson and Mr Holmes, shall I show them in?" Harrison asked, as we could see the array of electric lightbulbs festooned around the dressing mirror inside.

"Oh yes, please do, Mr Harrison, I have waited for a very long time to make their personal acquaintance!" I had only a vague recollection of how Miss Adler's voice sounded, but the sweet, feminine tone had an unmistakable American intonation to it.

As Harrison turned to us waiting in the corridor, I distinctly heard a male voice, which I presumed to be that of Mr Norton, the Solicitor-General. "Irene, dear, are you sure it was a good idea to invite them? You do remember the previous circumstances in which we tangled with Holmes?" It was a strong, deep voice indicating a man of some physical strength, not the image that Holmes had conjured for me when he had become the sole witness to the Nortons' brief marriage ceremony at the tiny church of St Monica in Edgeware Road, in March 1888.

"Of course! These are far more pleasant times in which to meet the world's greatest detective and his sterling biographer. After all, we have nothing to hide these days! I am a solicitor-general's wife, and an opera singer, why should I fear to meet the one man who was my intriguing equal in my former wild days?" Mrs Norton trilled, clearly delighted by the prospect of being reunited with Holmes. I was secretly pleased that she should also remember *my* existence!

Harrison pulled the door open and we gained entry. Irene Adler had clearly lost little if any of her beauty. Perhaps a little colouring in the hair to trick the march of time, but she retained a peerless complexion enhanced only by her sparing use of cosmetics, some mascara and lipstick. She wore an evening gown of blue silk trimmed in lace, very much in the old Victorian style, yet it flattered her still slender figure. It was no wonder that Mr Norton, standing as tall as Holmes, a little taller than I, possessed of broad shoulders, a full, healthy face, dark bushy hair and flashing brown eyes, should have his hand around his wife's waist in a rather possessive manner.

Holmes boldly stepped forward and took Mrs Norton's proffered hand in his. He appeared to breathe in the scent of her perfume which I could faintly discern was of damask rose, and then kissed her fingers. Such confidence I had not seen in my old friend! Women he regarded as a necessary encumbrance in his work, but I should have known, 'The Woman' was the true exception to the rule in his mind. "Miss Adler, or should I say, Mrs Norton? What a delight to finally meet you in my own appearance! I was so surprised to receive your invitation!"

Holmes declared, his grey eyes dancing brightly.

She giggled coyly as schoolgirls are wont to do, shrinking back a little, but the smile beamed from her lips and eyes as if she had found a long lost friend. Mrs Norton clapped her immaculately manicured hands, "And you, Sherlock Holmes, at last to know we are on the same side! I must give you my belated thanks for your wise dealings with His Majesty of Bohemia. For a royal ruler, he was somewhat petty in sending you after me. I had long lost affection for him after my term in Warsaw, and yet he was so impudent in his reaction to my leaving him. Anyway, it is all ancient history now. Do please, introduce me to your friend, the wonderful Watson who writes so thrillingly of your adventures!"

I felt, perhaps shamefully, rather suspicious of their familiarity, especially as Mr Norton seemed rather ill at ease with our presence as he had verbalised to his wife earlier. Holmes, as ever, the consummate actor — have I not often remarked in my writings that the stage lost a very fine one when Sherlock Holmes chose the detection of crime as his life's work? — introduced me with a flourish of his hand, "This is my trusted right arm, Dr John Watson, who indeed makes my chronicles of observation and deduction sound far more like a chapbook than a lecture in the most important forensic method ever to be brought to the general public! But he does so very gallantly!" I physically winced at Holmes' flattery, but he continued regardless, "Watson, 'The Woman' herself, Miss Irene Adler!"

The lady held out her hand and I shook it somewhat stiffly to my chagrin. I attempted to recover myself in my reply, "Good evening, Miss Adler, I hope tonight's performance will be successful for you."

"Oh indeed it shall, Dr Watson, I just had a peek through the curtains on the main stage and the theatre is very busy! My audience have been very loyal over all these years, and some have been kind enough to follow my daughter's musical career also. Have you heard of her work? She is becoming a very successful concert pianist!" she said brightly.

Before I could comment on the fact that music was more Holmes' interest than mine, my old friend interrupted, "Is she here? I should so like to meet her!" The excitement in his voice was palpable.

Mrs Norton looked round at her husband, some unspoken communication passing between them. Godfrey Norton spoke up as he moved past myself and Holmes, "Our daughter is indeed in the vicinity, Mr Holmes, I shall go and fetch her." He swiftly made his exit leaving the three of us together.

"Well, Miss Adler, the theatre manager is very much your admirer; he tells us you are to reprise some of your Gilbert & Sullivan work tonight! Their light operettas are not to my taste, but I am sure you will remedy that. Are you going to present your 'Pippo'? Rossini's overtures are rather infectious! *The Thieving*

Magpie', Watson, Pippo is a serving boy, but the libretto was written specifically for a contralto. Miss Adler's performance at La Scala was so well-received!" Holmes chattered.

"Oh now, you flatter me, Mr Holmes, I did know you had seen that!" she said, her cheeks colouring.

"Ah, indeed, and years later I cursed my foolishness of not remembering you being perfectly at home in male clothing after our rather bizarre first meeting! But all is forgiven and forgotten, and here, you have a daughter too, if she is as charming and talented as her mother, she will have the finest reputation as a musician after Neruda, now in her seventies and still famed for her heavenly violin-playing!" he said.

I was beginning to feel surplus to requirements; Holmes' taste in music was far more eclectic than mine, where I would be happy listening to a military band in Regent's Park, he would be found at the Alhambra, cooing to himself over the orchestration of a ballet, or indeed, I could enjoy some of Mr Oscar Wilde's witty stage plays, whereas

Holmes would seek out amateur productions of Shakespeare if he happened to know one of the actors. It was then, much to my relief that Mr Norton returned with a tall, pretty girl possessed of the same ebony locks and bright blue eyes as that of her mother.

"Mr Holmes, Dr Watson, may I present our talented little piano diva, Sophie Estella Norton," Godfrey said with the tone of a proud father.

I was rather astounded when she turned to me at first, holding out her hand, "Dr Watson, pleased to make your acquaintance, I do follow your excellent case reports, they are so exciting, one finds it hard to believe such terrible and strange things can happen in our world!" she trilled, her voice very definitely English.

"Thank you, Miss Norton, I was not fully aware of exactly how popular the stories of our adventures had become! The editor of the Strand Magazine sometimes wishes there were yet more sensational happenings for Holmes to investigate and me to record! But, thankfully there are many things that the ordinary person does not see, and it is better that they remain blissfully unaware of the unsavoury characters that reside in this world. All credit to my good friend here that he ensures the machinations of such individuals seldom see the light of day," I told her, as she nodded intently.

Miss Norton then turned her attention to my friend; Holmes was entranced as he took both her hands in his and looked at her in wonderment as if she was a fairytale creature who had just stepped out of a tale by Jacob Grimm. She spoke after a brief silence, "And the great detective himself, Mr Sherlock Holmes! I feel as if I already know everything about you. My mother has been a lifetime admirer of yours!"

"And I of hers, my dear Miss Norton. So, you were born here in England, yes? And went to a boarding school, though not far, Kent perhaps?" Holmes began, causing me to understand the reason for his intense gaze upon the daughter of his erstwhile acquaintance. He was, as ever, 'observing' in order to 'deduce'.

The girl gasped in surprise, clearly having never experienced one of Holmes' social diagnoses.

"Oh Mr Holmes! You are as clever as mother always said! How did you know these things?"

"Observation, my dear Sophie, and a lifetime's study of accents and dialects. Your mother, being born American, uses many little phrases and idioms which are not common in the speech of Britons, but you clearly do not. There is a slight trace of southern English in your accent; you have the deportment of a young lady who has been taught to be aware of such things, all marks of a boarding school education in Kent or somewhere similarly close to London. Also, you described Watson's writings as 'case reports', such a phrase you would have heard your father use, and one which is common in English legal parlance, which you would not have used if you had been brought up in the United States," Holmes explained. His reasoning made perfect sense, and yet I still had not learned his tricks even after several decades of close friendship.

Miss Norton shrieked with delight, "Wonderful! Wonderful, Mr Holmes! And my interest in the law is not only because of my father's position, but also as my fiancé has aspirations to be called to the bar one day! You must meet him!" she pulled out of Holmes' grasp and turned to the still open door, "James! James, come here a moment!" she called. Soon a young, fair-haired man appeared. He was attired in a dinner suit, but seemed uncomfortable in grand clothes, as he pulled at his stiff collar with his finger. When he saw us, he appeared to shrink back into the doorframe. Miss Norton pulled her fiancé into the room, "James, I want you to meet the great Sherlock Holmes, the most famous detective of our age and the last!" she said enthusiastically.

Master Doyle's eyes lit upon Holmes first; he straightened himself and shook Holmes' hand, "Pleased to meet you, sir, I am called James Doyle, a recent graduate from Fitzwilliam College, Cambridge."

Again, Holmes drank in every detail of this new arrival with the eyes of a hunting hawk sizing up its prey before he spoke. To others it was a mere second of time, but my friend's superior faculties processed a thousand details at once. "Yes, yes, but you were indeed brought up in Switzerland with an English tutor, yet some intonations betray your southern Irish ancestry, your father and grandfather, I believe? Your voice is very polished, as one would expect from a Cambridge don, but your mother's first language being German, your word construction reflects your fluency in it first, before English."

The young Irishman's eyes widened, "Amazing, Mr Holmes! And how did you arrive at such a conclusion?"

"My dear chap, you can see that your first tongue was German, you are not so aware of the orthography of it as you are of English which was learned later. You said 'I am called James' — a native English speaker would not use such a construction — but translate it back to German, *Ich heiße*, I am named, or I am called, and it makes perfect sense. Guten abend, wie geht es ihnen?" Holmes concluded, his German accent flawless.

"Ah ha, Sprechen Sie auch Deutsch! Danke schön, und Sie?" replied Master Doyle, as if suddenly comfortable in his mother tongue.

"Sehr gut, Mein Herr!" Holmes added.

"Would that we had you as a tutor at Cambridge, how we could have benefited from your deductive reasoning!" James Doyle exclaimed.

Indeed, but what school of learning would ever contend with Holmes' unconventional ways and his sometimes undisguised contempt for both the police force and the British legal system? I mused.

Holmes grinned and waved his hand dismissively, "Now, how is your Irish Gaelic?" he asked, presumably about to dazzle the company with his knowledge of the Celtic tongue. However, Master Norton was prevented from replying directly as we were suddenly joined by another. I had not even heard the sound of the wheelchair approach, but behind us, aided by Mr Harrison, who pushed the green room door wide, arrived a gruff and garrulous grey-haired man with a wiry beard, thick tortoiseshell-patterned spectacles which sat upon a sharp, rather hooked nose. His dress was very fine, including an expensive tweed coat with black velvet collar detailing, and, tied at his throat was a blue Angora wool scarf. As he opened his mouth it was evident that he was a native of the Emerald Isle, "Not as good as it should be for the son of an Irishman! So, you're the great Sherlock Holmes, eh? I'm the boy's father, right here!"

Mrs Norton stepped forward, her dress rustling as she moved, "Mr Doyle senior, so you did decide to come after all? Well, we're very glad to have you here! Everyone, this is Mr Seumas Doyle, former mountaineer and explorer," she said, offering her hand to old Doyle who reluctantly shook it.

I recalled once hearing of Doyle in his role as an Irish politician and decided to re-join the conversation using this knowledge, "So, Mr Doyle, I hear you're a mountaineer, and weren't you in Lord Palmerston's government? I remember my father talking about you."

"That I was, Dr Watson, and member for Carlow! That was surely before you were born! But it's the mountains I loved best," old Doyle replied, his gruff tone a little less unpleasant than a few moments ago.

Holmes evidently had heard of Master Doyle's father too, as he spoke, turning to the wheelchair-bound gentleman, "And so your love of mountains led you to found the Alpine Club in 1857, and your published guide was of great use to me even twenty-some years later during my little sojourn in Europe. Did you encounter many bears while you were in Canada, Mr Doyle? I hear they are becoming very dangerous to the human settlements in the Rockies. And is the Athabasca Glacier so much different from those in Switzerland?"

"So, you *do* do your homework, Mr Holmes! Yes, those grizzlies! Why they have the boldness to come right up to people's cabins and rifle their bins for scraps of food, so they do! And I have to admit, I was more interested in Canadian flora on the Palliser Expedition than the glaciers. My colleague Hector was almost obsessed with compiling our book on the native flowers, that fair took up our time entirely! But I'm an old man now, an accident robbed me of the pleasure some years ago, so it did!" old Doyle growled, gripping the arms of the chair.

I felt some pity that such an active man was now forced to spend his final years in such a sedentary existence. Unsure as to the nature of his disability, I ventured, "What befell you, Mr Doyle? A fall while on an expedition?"

"Aye, scaling a sheer rockface in winter, the pins were in snow rather than the rock itself and came loose, and I fell a great distance. I lay for hours in agony, knowing my legs were broken. Luckily some other climbers came to my rescue. The ice got into my joints and I had gangrene, so the Swiss surgeon at the hospital where my late wife worked had both my legs amputated!" old Doyle elaborated. I was suddenly reminded of the brutal and bloody sights to which I had been witness in Afghanistan. The old man was surely possessed of an iron will to live through such a tragedy. He seemed to realise I would understand as he continued, holding my gaze in his, "But that surgeon was a genius, he had artificial legs made for me, so I could retain some dignity and walk a little, but now I rely on this chair," Doyle said, patting the pneumatic tyres, "So the mountains will have to fair without me!"

"Well sir, having seen servicemen with lesser injuries succumb to madness, you appear to cope admirably! It must be so galling for one who has led such an active life!" I said, beginning to admire the grey-haired Irishman.

"T'is true, but my brain is as sharp as ever, and yer man can still range about on the mountains of the mind!" old Doyle waved his hand as if outlining an imagined line of peaks. "But now, I must gain my position for the performance. James! Are you joining yer old father or staying with yer young colleen?" he said, turning to his son.

James looked sheepishly at the company present, clearly overwhelmed, until Sophie surreptitiously slipped her hand into his. "Do excuse me, sir, but I'll sit with Sophie," was his quiet reply.

"Bah! Very well! Harrison! Conduct me to the stalls, if you please!" he barked, as the theatre manager had remained just outside the door. Smiling apologetically, Harrison, his grip tightly on the chair's handles, pulled old Doyle back into the corridor and wheeled him away in the direction of the main auditorium.

An awkward silence prevailed for a moment until Mrs Norton spoke, "I'm afraid I'll have to shoo you all out now, I must attend to my vocal exercises.

But thank you, again, Dr Watson ... Sherlock, for accepting my invitation." She gave Holmes a long look with her sapphire eyes; he seemed unable to tear himself away from her, temporarily frozen as the Greek heroes were by the Gorgon. I grabbed Holmes by the arm and commented that the performance was due to start in ten minutes, breaking the spell. I heard Sophie Norton tell her fiancé that she would join him in a moment. We walked along the corridor, James Doyle having scuttled ahead of us. Holmes said nothing, but apart from the almost lunatic grin on his lips, he appeared to be puzzling over the recent conversation.

Sophie hoped that James' neat dress and chivalrous manners might have swayed her mother's opinion of the previous evening. She so wished this night to go well, knowing that so many of Irene's friends and supporters were in the audience waiting for her at that moment. "Mother, have we settled our differences now? James is no brawler; he's a gentleman is he not?" she said sweetly, twisting her handkerchief in her fingers which she had lately pulled out of her clutch bag, made of the same purple silk as her gown.

Irene was now seated at the mirror, patting her nose with a powder puff. Her expression suddenly changed to one of surprise, "Sophie, once a man reveals his true self it is very hard to trust his public persona! I am still not sure you know James as well as you think! And Mr Doyle Senior is such a… well, such a boorish person!"

Sophie's mouth gaped open; she could hardly believe it, "Mother! Don't be such a snob! You were perfectly happy to accept James knowing he was a Cambridge student, and yet just one little slip is all it takes to cause you to dislike him! As for his father, Seumas is an old man! He is very angry about his accident, though he blusters that it is nothing, he misses being so active! You cannot grudge the man his feelings surely? Do not spoil my happiness just because your career as at an end!" She did not wait for a reply but stormed out of the green room in a flash of silks.

Irene leapt to her feet and ran to the door. It was no use. *So she does wish me out of her life! The girl has gone mad! What is this world coming to?* She thought. But there was little time for negativity on this night of all nights! She straightened her spine and took a deep breath, "No, no, I must cast it from my mind, and put on a performance worthy of the Prima Donna of Warsaw!"

Holmes and I remained unaware of this little spat as Miss Norton had contrived to find a different route to the auditorium. We crossed near the orchestra pit where the usual cacophony of sounds emanated from the various musicians tuning their instruments. I looked at my friend, able to see his expression as the house lights were still fully lit. "Holmes, you look puzzled, I can almost hear the internal cogs turning, upon what are you pondering now?"

"Just something odd. It is always the trifles, Watson, the merest slip which reveals the truth, hmm," he muttered, placing his finger on his lips.

"Pray elaborate, then Holmes! I do hate when you keep me on tenterhooks like this!" I whispered loudly.

"Perhaps it is the man's age, his mind is addled, but his assertion that he is in full possession of his mental faculties make me wonder. You know I have always told you I only keep in my mind the essential facts for the execution of my scientific methods, and some things, which you consider to be common knowledge, are of no interest to me, yet any man of a general education may be acquainted with such facts…" he drifted back into that vast mental archive he often inhabited and rubbed his forehead with his long fingers as if trying to retrieve a missing link in his knowledge.

I have had long experience of Holmes in this pensive mood, and though I had tolerated it for many years, perhaps my broken repose was still having an effect on my own attitude. "Yes, yes, come now, in what riddles are you talking?" I snapped.

"Canadian wildlife, Watson." He stopped, and after shaking his head several times exclaimed, "Oh! I shall have to satisfy myself, excuse me, I shan't be a moment!" with that he dashed off, like the hare in Aesop's fable, up the stairs of the stalls to the main exit level.

"But Holmes! The performance is about to start!" I called, then realised the other patrons were looking askance at me. I muttered to myself, "The man still has the capacity to infuriate me after all these years! What can have got into him? He appears more animated than I have ever seen him towards any of womankind in greeting Mrs Norton and her child, and now he babbles about wildlife and a man's senility!" Perhaps my friend had finally begun to lose his senses after all. I sighed wearily and found my seat, which happened to be next to Godfrey Norton. He smiled politely, which I returned, but gave no explanation for Holmes' impetuous behaviour.

- 3 -

By the time Holmes returned from his mysterious jaunt, the theatre was almost full. The house lights had not been dimmed, but the orchestra was silent. Miss Sophie Norton appeared to be having difficulty breathing, but was very soon attended by her maid, who came from the direction of the theatre bar with a tray containing a water jug, two glass tumblers and a dark brown medicine bottle. At the sight of the familiar container, I guessed at once that the young lady was suffering from some chronic condition. Mr Doyle Snr's wheelchair was placed at the end of the row next to his son, but Miss Norton eased herself to a standing position while leaning heavily on the arms of the red plush seat. Mr Norton whispered to her, "Are you alright, my dear?"

"Yes Father, look, Mary's brought my tincture, I shall be quite well in a moment!" Miss Norton replied, in stilted words.

The maid deftly supported the salver with her right arm and poured water into both tumblers with her left hand. She then measured a few drops from the medicine bottle into one tumbler. Miss Norton picked it up and swirled the glass to mix what I speculated was a tincture of Digitalis, the common Foxglove, which physicians were now prescribing for patients suffering weak or fluttering hearts. She sipped with apparent relief, but suddenly old Doyle cried out in agony. He lunged to the right, but in an attempt to steady himself, knocked into the maid with his elbow.

"Oh dear, Mr Doyle!" Mary Knox exclaimed, as the water in the other tumbler splashed out onto the salver.

"What's the matter, Father, what ails you?" James Doyle gasped.

The old grampus muttered, "Ah, 'tis nothing, 'tis the phantom pains that are on me! Just let me settle meself in this old chair!"

"Mary! That other glass was for mother!" Miss Doyle exclaimed impatiently, as her servant pulled a dishcloth from her apron pocket and mopped up the excess liquid on the tray.

"I'm sorry Miss Sophie, but Mr Doyle jogged my arm! I'll pour another, we have time, I'm sure!" poor Mary was flustered.

"Now, now, ladies, no harm done, my old bones are the cross I have to bear. Come, let me refill the tumbler for Mrs Norton!" old Doyle offered, his hand stretching out to the tray.

"Oh no, I didn't mean… it's not for you to do that, sir, let me put the tray down and start again!" Mary said, grasping the tray with both hands, fearing it would be upset completely with the unnecessary interference.

Young James tried to restrain his father from further unwelcome 'help', but I could clearly see his large hand close round the handle of the jug. Miss Norton turned directly towards her maid and her fiancé, and I could no longer see very clearly the progress of events. Mr Norton hissed at his daughter, "Do come on, Sophie, you promised your mother a glass of water!"

I distinctly heard Sophie's voice again, directed at one of the three she faced, "That's my tincture, not the water, oh please, do leave it!"

The maid took charge of the situation and whisked the tray away from them, leaving Miss Norton and James Doyle to regain their seats. Mary placed the tray down on the steps leading to the stage just as Mrs Norton poked her head round the curtain. Mary handed her the freshly-filled tumbler and Mrs Norton began to sip immediately as if desperately thirsty. She disappeared back on stage and the maid disappeared through the right-hand exit with the tray.

What a strange little to-do! I stole a glance at Holmes who had apparently been oblivious and had his attention focused entirely on the stage. The lights dimmed, a spotlight trained on the centre of the stage whereupon Mr Harrison stepped out from behind the curtains.

"Ladies and gentlemen, opera-lovers," he began, in the booming voice of a practised master of ceremonies, "Tonight the management of the Leicester Square Theatre is very proud to present the final stage performance of a diva from across the Atlantic who some twenty years ago adopted England as her home; her great career began in Madison

Square Garden, New York City, and culminated in a highly successful term as the Prima Donna of the Warsaw Opera, Poland. Therefore we welcome to the stage, singing that light favourite from our own Messrs Gilbert and Sullivan's operetta, *The Mikado*, "Katisha's Song"! Please, show your appreciation for Miss Irene Adler!"

There was a roar of appreciation and thunderous clapping as the curtains pulled back and Irene Adler stepped into the pool of golden light which highlighted the glittering sequins on her gown and her hair ornaments. Her accompanist sat at a grand piano, dressed in a dinner suit complete with tailcoat. He played a few stirring opening chords and the audience quietened. Mrs Norton stood, looking around, lacking the confidence I had earlier noted in her demeanour. She began to speak, her American accent more pronounced, "Just before I begin this, my absolute apple-pie favourite, I want to thank you all for being here and demonstrating your loyalty and kindness to me as a stage artist all these years. When I stood up to sing back in New York at the age of eighteen, I was shaking like a leaf, and tonight…" she hesitated, I could see her hands, though covered in gorgeous silk opera gloves, were visibly shaking. She took several deep breaths and continued, "Tonight, a quarter of a century later, I am as nervous as I was then!" Mrs Norton put a hand to her upper chest as if she was in pain. I feared that the excitement of the occasion had quite overcome her. Then her eyes lit on Holmes who leapt to his feet and began to applaud again.

"Begin, Miss Adler, we await your pleasure!" he called, his superior tones carrying across the auditorium. He turned, clapping all the more furiously; the audience joined in, clearly keen that their heroine should not fear any ill-judgement from them.

Irene's cheeks flushed red under her powder, and she smiled gratefully, "Thank you, dear Sherlock Holmes! Now, as Mr Harrison announced, I will sing "Katisha's Song" from *The Mikado*."

The pianist began to play the opening bars of the Gilbert & Sullivan ditty which had made this singer famous. Irene visibly steeled herself and right on cue the first sonorous notes of the contralto's voice shone out into the air. She truly was a star. Holmes may not have been keen on G&S, but he appeared rapt in the performance, his grey eyes glittering with emotion. This woman did mean more to him than all the others. She seemed to kindle some intense, almost elemental feeling in my old friend which no-one else had ever succeeded in doing. For a man who openly despised romance, Holmes appeared to have had some sort of siren spell cast upon him, as the legendary spirits tempted Odysseus to his death in Homer's dramatic tale.

But alas, the spell was suddenly broken when Irene gasped in the middle of her aria, clutched her left arm and collapsed to the ground. Her daughter squealed in horror, James flung his arms around Sophie to restrain her from running onstage. Holmes, Mr Norton and I were all on our feet, but my friend reached the lady first. I saw him slip his arms around her limp shoulders and shake her gently, "Irene, the only woman to defeat me! Hold on, hold on, good old Watson's here, he'll help you, I promise!"

Never have I heard Holmes sound frightened, but there, in a hubbub of confusion, he had lost all composure. He leaned close to her and I saw his lips move. It was a question meant for the lady alone, but by this time I stood above them, Godfrey Norton just trailing behind me.

Irene's eyelids flickered for a moment, and replied in a cracked voice, "Oh Sherlock! No, she is not, would that she had been!" With that she slumped again in his arms.

Godfrey furiously pushed me aside and grabbed Holmes by the shoulders, his larger form easily managing to send my friend sprawling in an ungainly manner across the stage. "Out of my way, Holmes, let me be with my wife!" he roared.

Mr Harrison was already pulling on the mechanism to close the curtains, but I fear some of the audience would have seen this angry exchange. I had to be firm. I crouched beside Mr Norton and said as calmly as I could, "Mr Norton... Godfrey, I'm sorry, but I'm a medical doctor, I can help your wife if you'll just let me attend to her."

The man was fighting back his own tears as he looked into my face. "I-I'm sorry, old boy, yes, you must help her, please, I'm sorry!" Godfrey pulled himself to his feet.

The accompanist, who had uttered an oath when Irene collapsed now proved useful as he skirted around the piano, put his arm across Godfrey's back and steered him offstage. "Come on, Godfrey, she's in the hands of an expert, let's leave him to it, eh?"

I saw that Irene's pallor was immediately turning from a healthy pink to a sallow blue- grey. Putting my hand below her nostrils I could feel no breath. I quickly checked the carotid pulse below her ear, but to my horror there was only the weakest of responses. "Mary! Mary, send for an ambulance!" I bawled as I saw the little maid appear from the wings. She scuttled off to Mr Harrison's office where there would be a telephone.

Holmes appeared again, pushing his ruffled hair out of his eyes. His face was as ghostly as that of his admired lady friend. "Watson, old friend, will she...?" he could not bring himself to speculate further.

"I don't know, Holmes, I simply don't know. I suspect the nearest place is St. Bart's, you know they have expert surgeons, if it's some kind of seizure, they'll know what to do, I'm sure!" I replied, foolishly promising the equivalent of the moon.

Holmes smiled weakly. He did not argue, he simply stared down at her, gulping back a sob. *Dear Heavens, did he really care so much for her?* I thought. I pulled off my evening jacket and rolled it into a makeshift pillow which I put under Irene's head. Her eyes were closed. She lay like an expensive china doll that had been dropped by a spoilt child, her dress crumpled beneath her, one arm twisted awkwardly, which I gently straightened and draped over her waist. Mary came rushing back.

"They said they will come as soon as they can, Dr Watson, they're coming from St Bartholomew's, half an hour maybe they said!" she gasped. "I told them Mrs Norton had collapsed and that she wasn't getting up. They know it's serious!"

"Very good, Mary, well done. Can you go and fetch a blanket or shawl from somewhere to keep your mistress warm?" I instructed, not wishing the girl to have to stand and gawp at her employer in such a distressing condition.   Mary nodded and dashed off again.

"Holmes,   I'm   sorry,   I   can't   promise anything…" I stopped, I did not wish to tell him to prepare himself for the worst. I knew that his own mother's death still caused him grief and anger so many years after the event, so how would he cope with the demise of 'The Woman'?   His perhaps… dearest enemy?

4

It seemed hours had passed since Joseph Harrison had made the announcement that Miss Adler had taken ill and the performance would have to be postponed. Sophie shook uncontrollably, burying her head in James' shoulder. He could only hold her close and whisper platitudes to calm her down, his lips brushing her forehead every so often to assure her of his presence. His father had turned his wheelchair to face the auditorium, mainly to prevent himself being an obstacle to the other members of the audience as they filed out. James wondered at his father's expression; it was one of puzzlement, punctuated with strange and grotesque grimaces. James realised that just as he had been starkly reminded of his mother's death, so his father was suffering at the memories of losing his young wife. Helena Doyle, née Reinshagen, was only forty-five years old, but had caught enteric fever from one of the patients at the hospital where she worked. James hoped against hope that Irene's collapse had merely been a nervous fit, nothing more, but Sophie's raking sobs made him wonder if some supernatural agency had given his fiancée certainty about her mother's fate.

They had heard voices behind the curtain, detected movement, likely the ambulance driver and the porter, come to collect Mrs Norton. A moment later Sherlock Holmes slipped from behind the curtains and walked slowly down the steps. Sophie looked up and wiped her eyes, "Oh! Mr Holmes, is my mother going to be alright?" she asked, attempting to sound cheerful.

James saw the detective's face, it was pale, the skin drawn around reddened eyes which had evidently shed tears. He knew from what Sophie told him that Mrs Norton and Mr Holmes had a great mutual admiration, thus it was no surprise that he too should be overcome with emotion.

Holmes strode across to them and crouched beside Sophie. He put his hand upon hers and looked intently into her face, "My dear child, I… I have to tell you the truth. Your mother is dead. Watson believes she has had a heart attack, he and your father have gone in the ambulance to hospital, but it's too late, I'm afraid."

Sophie howled, "No! Not mother, no! It can't be true, I am the one who has a weak heart, not mother, she was as lively as a bird!" Fresh tears drenched her cheeks. She turned to her fiancé and seized his arms, "Oh James, James, I wished her dead yesterday! I didn't mean it, I didn't!"

The young Irishman replied in as soothing a tone as he could muster, "Mo chroí, I know you didn't! These things just happen, no-one knows why! I'm so sorry, I'm sure Dr Watson did his best!"

Holmes got to his feet. His jacket and coat were missing somewhere. He pulled the cravat from about his collar. "Indeed, Master Doyle, my old friend tried to revive her, but it was very sudden. I just wish… I wish it had not been like this." Holmes glanced upwards as if he could not bear to meet their gazes. He continued wistfully, "For all Irene Adler's incorrigible behaviour in her youth, she was the brightest and best of all the fair sex and I would never have wished to see her so cruelly taken from the world."

Seumas Doyle coughed, "Don't you remember your Latin, Mr Holmes? Pale death strikes her hoof both at the doors of paupers and kings! You think your Miss Adler something special that she should be spared what is common to us all in the end?" James was horrified at his father's harshness.

"You are very hard-hearted, Mr Doyle. Did you not lose your own wife recently? Is this how your grief manifests itself in bitterness at the world?" Holmes replied gently.

Seumas shifted in his wheelchair and pulled at his scarf, "Bitter? Nothing of the sort! I am a realist, Mr Holmes. As a mountaineer I faced death often and defied it often, but I saw so many who lost their lives, I know one day it will come to me, as it so nearly did at the bottom of that waterfall!"

Holmes turned and strode away until he reached the edge of the front stalls. Immediately the word 'waterfall' had broken through the cloud of his grief. *Waterfall? You fell from a cliff face, Mr Doyle, not a waterfall, unless your memory truly is beginning to fail you!* "The girl is the one with the weak heart, yet her dear mother is the one who takes a heart attack. She never

ever had any such condition! I need more data, more data indeed!" Holmes whispered to himself. He strode up the aisle, slipping his hand into his waistcoat pocket and producing a small notebook with a stub of pencil attached to the spine by means of a large paperclip. He jumped into an empty seat and began scribbling with purpose.

"I must get some air, James, I cannot bear it any more, where is Mary?" Sophie muttered.

"Let's go and find her, I think she's been helping Dr Watson," James replied. They stood up and walked to the exit leading backstage.

The next time Holmes looked up he realised he was alone. He sprinted down the aisle, up the steps to the stage and turned the crank-wheel in the wings to draw back the curtains. "Ah, so, Mary did *not* return the tray to the bar, of course she wouldn't, it was a salver from the house!" he exclaimed, spotting the silver tray, containing both tumblers and the water jug, in the corner just by the right-hand stage entrance. Retrieving a jeweller's loupe from his other waistcoat pocket, Holmes prostrated himself in front of the tray. He squinted at the glassware through the loupe, keeping his hands away from their surfaces. *Fingerprints, and many of them!* Mary had surely taken the medicine bottle with her, knowing its importance to her young mistress. There was very little water in either the tumblers or the jug. Holmes leaned his face over each one in turn and sniffed carefully. A grin of realisation swept across his lips. "Ah-ha, yes! *Both* glasses. *And* it would have the opposite effect on a healthy person! Eureka, as Archimedes said!" Holmes could not help speaking aloud. He sprang to his feet, jumped off the stage and landed neatly just beside the edge of the orchestra pit.

Holmes approached the seats which he, Watson, the Nortons and the Doyles had so recently occupied. He dropped again to his knees and crawled up to the point where Sophie had stood while Mary presented her with her tincture. He spread his fingers across the deep pile carpet, feeling the still wet patch from the spilled water.

A voice from above startled him, "My dear Holmes, what are you doing on the floor? I thought you would come down to the hospital."

"Ah, Watson," Holmes began, continuing his investigations, "I am examining the scene of the crime, as is my wont! I am sure you will be able to obtain a copy of the post mortem examination to confirm my findings, but the body of evidence is right here in this theatre!"

When I returned from the hospital after briefing the surgeon, I was, in one way, unsurprised to find Holmes on his knees poking his head under the seat where Miss Norton had been sitting. "Are you saying that Mrs Norton's death was not natural, Holmes? She had a heart attack, surely that can happen at any time? She was, after all, no longer *young*." I commented, hoping desperately that this sounded merely logical and not callous.

Holmes scrambled quickly to his feet, his fifty-six years causing not a jot of difference to his agility. He patted my shoulder in the usual way before he explained a case in 'layman's terms', but I was shocked that he could think what had begun as a delight to him the day before, was now something more sinister. "Watson, you are a medical man, and yes, you are correct, but in this case the evidence points to a heart attack induced by an unnatural element."

His tone on the word 'unnatural' was deeper, telling me that he really believed that it was not Nature which was responsible for the Prima Donna's death. He turned and looked up at the circle. "See, Watson, some of Miss Adler's admirers have remained to hold vigil! Friends, you are all witnesses to a terrible crime – consider the evidence with us and we shall unmask our beloved contralto's killer together!"

5

Holmes was accustomed to an audience; like a seasoned thespian he put aside any feelings of grief for Irene Adler and proceeded to examine the elements of data which he believed comprised the evidence pointing to a suspicious death.

"Firstly, we saw Miss Adler appearing to be nervous on the stage, she herself attributing it to nerves, but no, she was shaking, short of breath, the signs of some internal agitation. Then she gripped her left arm before she fell. Watson, those are the symptoms of a heart attack are they not?" he said, clasping his hands behind his back.

I nodded vigorously; the classic pain from the clogged aorta suddenly sends a shooting pain across the veins in the chest so that it appears to come from the arm, resulting in misdiagnosis in a sufferer of a more minor cardiac episode.

"I maintain that something caused that to happen to her – and the cause came from that glass of water she drank before beginning her performance!" Holmes turned and pointed triumphantly towards the tumblers on the salver which were now in clear view at the edge of the stage. "Miss Adler… otherwise Mrs Norton was given the glass by the maid, who is likely to be completely innocent of all knowledge of the *real* contents of the liquid." He paused, as if waiting for the fact to sink into our heads, then strode back towards the stage until he was level with the tray. "You remember the little hiatus down here as the maid held the tray for Miss Sophie Norton to take her medicine? She was clearly agitated and believed she needed more." He continued. I glanced quickly at our fellow listeners who were leaning over the balcony of the circle. They were all nodding, indeed some of them, had they been looking down at the time would have had a clear view of the business with the water. Holmes turned to me, his grey eyes bright like the falcon ready to swoop, "Watson, what is Miss Norton's condition likely to be?"

"I did think about this earlier, Holmes, it is likely to be a preparation for the relief of an irregular heartbeat, in medical terms, arrhythmia. Digitalis, the chemical found in the humble foxglove has been shown through research to ease the condition. *That* is what Miss Norton's little ribbed bottle contained," I said firmly, continuing to look at the patrons in the circle, realising that Holmes knew very well from what Sophie Norton suffered, but was, like a barrister at the Old Bailey, laying out the evidence in turn for the benefit of the jury.

"Excellent, Watson! Now, what would happen if a perfectly healthy person were to ingest this substance?" Holmes asked as I turned my attention back to him.

But a healthy person would never knowingly… ah, of course! It dawned on me what Holmes was driving at, "Yes, yes, digitalis works to steady the heart rate of someone suffering arrhythmia, but it has the opposite effect on a healthy person — their heart rate is sent rushing away like a speeding train, and depending on the age of the person, may be fatal! Mrs Norton took some of the digitalis! But might it not have been a simple, but sorry error on the part of the poor maid?" I could never believe that any of the four involved in the little incident would knowingly poison Irene Adler.

Holmes cast me a look of consternation, yet again I had offered too prosaic an explanation. *Once you have eliminated the obvious…* I had fallen into the old trap, and here I was about to be shown the incredible truth which I never seemed able to discover without Holmes' aid. "No! Of course not, Watson, observe! Miss Norton had the same tumbler in her hand all the time while she was talking with Mary. There was only *one* tumbler on the tray with the jug. Mary was balancing the tray on her right arm and holding the medicine bottle with the other; *she* is left-handed. *Think*, Watson, you were sitting closer than I! Remember how Mr Doyle Snr called out in pain and shifted rapidly in his wheelchair, and Mary exclaimed he had jogged her arm. Then, keen to demonstrate he is a thoughtful sort, especially in front of Mr Norton, since Mrs Norton has already expressed her annoyance at him for his boorishness, Mr Seumas Doyle offers to pour the water afresh from the jug.

Master *James* Doyle is standing to Mary's left, as he moved from his seat when Sophie stood up, thus Mary is surrounded on all sides. Looking at the tumbler, the jug and now the medicine bottle, I can see there are at least four sets of fingerprints on them. Each person here had their hands on the items from the tray, so each — in the mind of a policeman at least —would be a suspect in poisoning my… our beloved performer, Irene Adler!" Holmes explained, gesturing with an upwards-pointed finger.

He strode back to the front row of the stalls, "But, as I have often repeated to the good doctor, my friends, it is dangerous to theorise without sufficient evidence — consider the material I observed on the floor here where Mary placed the tray for a moment!" I had not even noticed that Holmes had these insignificant items in his handkerchief, which he now produced carefully from his waistcoat pocket. "A long black strand of hair — Sophie's, which has simply fallen from her head. Why? Because head hair, as one learns in anatomy, is fixed to the scalp by means of tiny cells called follicles which secure the individual hair through pores, tiny holes in the skin. The aging man who is turning bald looks at his comb in despair as he sees many hairs held therein, as the dead tresses fall out. The anxious young woman might pull her hair out by its root, that is, the follicle;

and the little cluster of cells will be there, visible on the end of each strand. Sophie did not feel unduly anxious besides her usual concern for her heart, despite moments later exclaiming '*I wished her dead yesterday!*' when her mother succumbed. Those are the genuine words of a terrified child, not someone who truly meant such a vitriolic statement.

Secondly, a blue fragment of fluff, wool! Mr Doyle was seen wearing a blue woollen scarf which he did not remove until I returned but moments ago after Mrs Norton was taken to the hospital. He was close enough for the fluff to fall upon the floor by Mary's feet. You who were here heard Mr Doyle's apparently callous statement that death comes to all, high or low. Does that imply something more sinister or is it the tone of a man still wallowing in his own grief for his dead wife?

Thirdly, young Master James, a very bright young chap, but fearful that his student exploits have soured his relationship with his future mother-in-law, could he have had any evil intent towards her because she might force Sophie to break off the engagement? Ponder upon these things, ponder, evaluate and *deduce* shrewdly!" Holmes had left the unfolded handkerchief on the arm of the chair and clapped his hands together.

We were suddenly interrupted by the arrival of a constable. Seemingly familiar with our identities, he spoke rapidly, but calmly, "Mr Holmes, Dr Watson, Chief Inspector Lestrade sent me to tell you he's on his way. Says the police surgeon told him Mrs Norton's heart attack was brought on by digitalis poisoning."

Holmes nodded acknowledgement to the constable, "Thank you, Constable Kingsley," he turned to me and with fingers bridged together said, "See Watson? I knew the surgeon would confirm it! And our old friend Lestrade, two steps behind as ever!"

Lestrade, now promoted since I last encountered him, still wore his brown suit and bowler, now with a jaunty little feather in the hatband. Could the usually cantankerous officer have gained a little humour in his old age? He was as bluff and officious towards Holmes as ever, but pleasant towards me, like an old acquaintance long forgotten.

Constable Kingsley had been sent to fetch the others, and now old Doyle was positioned in his wheelchair near the centre aisle, with his son standing above him. Mr Norton stood at Lestrade's left side, I near Holmes who was now in a playful mood. He sat down with a flourish in the seat directly in front of Lestrade, "Well now, Chief Inspector, you say you have your murderer, please, enlighten us with your deductions!"

Lestrade puffed out his chest like a bold, but tiny robin redbreast, clearly resenting Holmes' levity, "Mr Holmes, with respect sir, I am an officer of the law, I am merely summarising the case for you as a matter of courtesy! I have indeed arrested my chief suspect for the murder of Mrs Irene Norton. If it hadn't been for Dr Watson insisting that the police surgeon checked for evidence of poisoning, this would have been a straight sudden death!"

Holmes applauded me, and I blushed, "Well done, Watson! I would have been very upset to think that anyone could have escaped justice because the Metropolitan Police imagined Mrs Norton's death to be a 'straight sudden death'! Do go on!"

Lestrade glared at him. I pitied the man for how Holmes played with him; it was that childish streak Holmes displayed when he felt he was addressing someone of lesser intelligence. However, what mortal's mind sparks like a lightning bolt and discerns things that ordinary eyes miss? None, but Sherlock Holmes. I cannot help my admiration for my friend, despite his sometimes insufferable pride in his own abilities. Lestrade eventually appeared to have summoned the will to bridle his tongue and continued, "But justice *is* done, Mr Holmes, justice is, and *will* be done! What we have here is the case of a young woman who has made a match that her mother doesn't quite like, and our modern miss decides to take matters into her own hand and do away with her mother and marry the young man of her fancy!"

Godfrey Norton bristled and stepped nearer Lestrade, "Surely you're not suggesting…?" he began, "Not Sophie! No! Now look here, Chief Inspector, you are premature in your judgements," he wagged his finger angrily in the officer's face, "Granted, Sophie had a few disagreements with my wife over her fiancé, James, but they were all down to nerves and high spirits! You can't possibly have arrested my daughter! Might I remind you I am the Solicitor-General?" his voice increased in volume and tension. He towered over Lestrade like the sparrowhawk who has come to challenge the little robin.

Lestrade retreated, motioning for Constable Kingsley to intervene, "Mr Norton, I know perfectly well who you are, and you should know that threatening a police officer could see you guilty of assault!"

Holmes guffawed "Come now, Lestrade, don't be such an old woman! Of course Mr Norton's annoyed, he's just lost his wife and you arrest his daughter! Where's your evidence, man?"

"Ahem, very well, I interviewed James and Seumas Doyle and Knox, the housemaid. They all saw what was happening when Miss Norton administered the poison to her mother's glass!"

Realising that Lestrade too had jumped to an altogether hasty conclusion, I could not help myself, "Chief inspector, you didn't interview me or Holmes, and did you talk to Miss Norton herself? I think you'll find, as my good friend often reminds me not to do, that you are theorising before you are in possession of all the facts! I do not think you should go any further before you hear our sides of the story, or rather, our observations!"

"I think your long acquaintance with Mr Holmes has made you as arrogant as 'im, Dr Watson! We spend so long dealing with criminals we know them when we see them! But, I suppose you are right," Lestrade replied in an offended tone. He sighed and turned back to Holmes, who had drawn his knees up to his chest and had his arms clasped around them like some hermit in a cave. Holmes beamed that same smile as when I gave him the opportunity to tell me his news after I returned from my patient in St. John's Wood. He leapt to his feet as if suddenly animated, and strode back towards the relevant seats in the front of the auditorium.

"Now, Watson, you can fill in anything I missed, as my attention was mainly on the stage, but you and I were seated here," he pointed to our seats, "Mr Norton was next to you, then Miss Norton, young Master Doyle, and Mr Seumas Doyle in his wheelchair, am I correct?" I looked at James Doyle for confirmation and he nodded.

"Yes Holmes, pray continue," I said.

"Mary Knox, the housemaid came past Mr Doyle with her tray which contained a water jug, two glass tumblers and a medicine bottle with a rubber stopper. She stood here – observe, there is still a damp patch where the water was spilled. Miss Norton stood up as soon as Mary entered, she was expecting her to come with the medicine, which you, Lestrade wrongly identify as poison; Miss Norton suffers from arrhythmia, that is an irregular heartbeat, and Watson correctly observed she would be on a course of digitalis to control her condition. *That* is what was in the bottle, and to her, a lifesaver, but to anyone else without the condition, life-threatening!" Holmes explained.

Lestrade opened his mouth in protest, but my friend raised his hand for silence, "Mary poured a glass of water for her mistress and measured the exact amount of her medicine into the water. Miss Norton correctly refers to it as a tincture, as the digitalis must be diluted in order to cause the desired effect for a sufferer of such a condition. She would know perfectly well that it was dangerous, which is why she trusted Mary to look after it for her. The housemaid would follow her young mistress's instructions to the letter, as she did in this case."

Lestrade finally got his words out as Holmes paused, "But surely Mr Holmes, surely Knox was in it with her then? Especially if they both knew how poisonous the stuff was to anyone else!"

Holmes sighed, closing his eyes and placing his clasped hands up to his chin, "Ah Chief Inspector, you always leap to the most obvious conclusion! Has it not registered with you yet in all the time we have known each other that you must discount every improbable suggestion subject to your evidence, and whatever remains, however bizarre, is the truth. You are too eager to have a body – *habeus corpus* – a suspect to present for every crime! So, bear with me, amateur though I am, but undisputedly the world's *only* consulting detective!" Lestrade rolled his eyes. He knew he was defeated.

Holmes took up the role of court counsel again, "Returning to my summary of events — Mr

Doyle suffers some sort of pain or discomfort and shifts in his chair; in doing so he makes contact with Mary's arm, which thus spills most of the second tumbler which Miss Norton had exclaimed, was for her mother. James, ever the dutiful son, leaps to his father's aid, but Doyle Snr recovers his composure very quickly. I suspect a man who has amputated limbs often suffers from 'phantom pains', the condition in which one imagines they still have the 'feeling' of the limb, am I right, Mr Doyle?" Holmes turned his attention to Seumas Doyle, who had sat impassive in his wheelchair throughout.

"'Tis true, Mr Holmes. It fairly works me up to feel my toes itch, and then to reach down and remember they are no longer there! Aye, that's what happened!" the old man replied in his Irish brogue.

"Indeed. Now when everyone crowded around the tray, and you, Mr Doyle, graciously offered to help poor Mary who was berated by Miss Norton, when all along you had caused the water to spill, yes?" Holmes did not once break his gaze with Doyle. I began to sense we were approaching the heart of the matter.

"How very kind to defend a servant! But then, you have roamed the world and realised that native people, treated as packhorses by some mountaineers, are the true guides and experts in that icy world, am I correct?" Holmes said, his voice remaining in that pleasant tone he used with most of his clients, "And indeed you reached out for the tumbler, but it was your son who poured the water. You then whispered to him to sit down that you could manage yourself, it aggravates you when even he is well-meaning, since you pride yourself on your ability to cope, despite your disability."

Mr Doyle nodded slowly and seemed relieved when Holmes turned back to me, "However, now Watson, I need your eyes to conclude this summary, but would you also go outside to the foyer and bring in Mary Knox? I asked her to wait as I wished her to give her observations to us all."

"At once, Holmes!" I replied, glad of something to do. Outside in the foyer which led to the bar, Mary Knox stood twisting her handkerchief in her fingers. "Mary, please, don't be frightened, Holmes wants you to join us," I said, touching her arm gently. The dark-skinned girl nodded her head in curtsey and followed me back into the auditorium.

Holmes beckoned us to where he stood. "Now, my old friend, what did you see when James returned to his seat?"

I closed my eyes a moment and attempted to gather my memories of the last few hours. Then, looking back at Holmes, I began to relate my story, "James sat down, Miss Norton was looking at him, just after she had put her original tumbler back on the tray. I looked at Mr Doyle and Mary holding the tray; to be truthful, I was admiring Mr Doyle's fortitude in trying to be as normal as possible for a man who no longer can walk. Mary looked up at me as if she sensed my gaze, and for one moment I looked back down and saw Mr Doyle's hand on the medicine bottle. I just assumed he was steadying it, but then now, perhaps… I don't know, Holmes! Mary took the tray away, then walked over to the stage, set the tray down on the steps and Mrs Norton opened the curtain. Mary gave her the tumbler from which I saw her immediately begin to drink as the curtain fell back.

Now I know as much as you do about what happened next!"

"Well done, Watson," Holmes commented, pacing up the aisle and partly addressing the patrons still in the circle, whom he insisted remain when Lestrade arrived. "You saw what I believed I had also. Several things concerned me about this case, even before Irene's terrible demise. When I am concerned, I gather data to satisfy those concerns. I am now almost in possession of all the facts, Chief Inspector, but first, I wish you all to listen to a story, a well-known tale concerning myself and… my greatest nemesis!

Many of you shared Watson's sorrow and horror at the tale he dubbed '*The Adventure of the Final Problem*', many years ago. He and many others of you believed I had perished along with Professor James Moriarty at the bottom of the Reichenbach Falls in Switzerland. I was later able to reveal my presence again, very much alive, but having lived in disguise in order to throw off Moriarty's henchmen who were equally devastated by the loss of their leader. I then set about dismantling his evil web once and for all, which, I can safely say I ultimately achieved," he smiled and shot a glance back at me.

"My memory of that fateful day is still as clear as ever, but perhaps in my relief at surviving a fall which in my case turned out to only be down to the next ridge, I was not fully aware of the fate of my rival, the man who was my equal, yet in everything, the dark, evil twin, twisting my desire for justice to an avaricious urge to control all that is wicked for his own ends! All I recall from that day was a horrible scream of a man who knows that his end is death. Then, as the bard himself said, the rest is silence. But I should have known, I should have guessed, that if I had been so blessed by some supernatural hand to have lived that day, then Moriarty's evil angels would also be taking care of him! I mentioned my concerns, and they arose after I realised I did not know enough about Canadian wildlife!"

It chilled me to the bone hearing Holmes recount what I had believed to be his final moments on earth, knowing that I had been deceived for three interminable years. Yet it had to be, our sorrows had to be endured to allow him the freedom to destroy the enemy he so sharply described as "a spider" at the centre of a nefarious web. The wildlife comment jolted me back to the present, "Yes Holmes, what on earth were you babbling about? That was after we left the Nortons in Irene's dressing room, and where did you run off to before the start of the concert?" I asked.

Holmes turned to Lestrade and waved a hand towards me, "What would I do without my foil? My Boswell!" Then he looked back, "Yes, Watson, I did leave the theatre, but only to pass a message on via the Baker Street division of the police force!"

Lestrade folded his arms in disgust, "Oh yes? Those street urchins! Mr Holmes's 'irregulars'! Ha! What could they do?"

"My dear Lestrade! You illustrate the point perfectly! My young friend Wiggins, now in his thirtieth year, and a street sweeper to trade, still holds greater knowledge of the capital's back streets than any policeman alive today. He has a whole new generation of young friends who, merely because they are children and they have only the gutters and alleyways for their beds, are virtually invisible to the public at large! That way they can spy and eavesdrop more effectively than any police inspector in his civilian clothes! Yes, it was Wiggins, I had seen him earlier in the evening. I sent him to the Reading Room at the British Museum, where I knew an old professor of zoology often visited for research until the last possible moment before closing. The professor and I often talked about predators and their means of stalking prey. It was very useful, especially in that Baskerville case! Why without Professor Rackham's knowledge, I would have had little idea of animal tracks!"

It was then Holmes brought his attention back to Mr Doyle. He crouched before the wheelchair and continued his little monologue, "Now Mr Doyle, I was well aware of your amazing explorations and your mountain books before I met you. Granted I was more interested in your descriptions of geology and topography than the wildlife, but something gnawed away at me after our conversation. Yes, I knew about the Canadian expedition, but I was so surprised to see you in this chair! I had no idea you had been injured so terribly. I even began to think that your accident had perhaps confused you, but then you so vehemently asserted your clear mind, thus I had to check my deduction with further evidence! You see, Mr Doyle, although there are indeed bears in Canada, and ones which do cause damage to human settlements as foolish people leave food out that attracts the beasts, the only bears in that country are black. *Black* bears, Mr Doyle, not 'grizzlies' as you described them.

'Grizzly' or brown bears are found in the United States of America, but not in the Northern provinces! I'm sorry Mr Doyle, but perhaps we are witnessing the onset of senility, as I could not expect such a mistake from an expert such as you!"

"I'm an old man, Mr Holmes, old people make mistakes!" Doyle groused.

Holmes stood up, his face impassive. He beckoned Mary forward. She dutifully stepped to his side, "Now, Mary, you have co-operated very well with both Chief Inspector Lestrade and myself, but please, tell us all exactly what you saw when everyone was crowding around the tray. Don't be afraid, the truth is the most important thing here!"

The little maid looked at Holmes and then down at her feet, "I – I was worried they would upset the tray completely and I would be blamed if there was broken glass! Mr Doyle reached out for the tumbler, but Master Doyle, that's James, held it steady on the tray in his left hand and he poured more water into it with his right. He put the jug back and said to Sophie, I mean, Miss Norton, "Stop worrying dear, I'm sure your mother will forgive you." Miss Norton was very upset because she'd had cross words with her mother just before curtain up. She kept saying "I do hope so, for both our sakes!" They were so busy looking at each other, and I busy listening, I couldn't help it, Miss Sophie is very kind to me, as are all the family, but she really does love Master Doyle, and she told me last night she would be heartbroken if Mrs Norton made her call off her engagement. Then I looked around and saw Dr Watson looking at me, then I looked down again and saw … oh, I'm sure I did…" she stopped, twisting her handkerchief into a knotted rag as she looked up at Holmes for reassurance.

He touched her shoulder in a kindly fashion, "Yes, you saw what you saw, tell me *exactly*! Your observation is the most vital piece of the whole puzzle!" Holmes' voice dropped to a whisper.

Mary shivered, but then took a deep breath and blurted out, "I saw Mr Doyle putting Miss Sophie's medicine bottle down on the tray and the stopper was in his other hand!" she pointed at the old man who gave no indication of surprise, "I think he must have put some of the tincture in the water meant for Mrs Norton!"

There were audible gasps from around the auditorium. Mr Norton came forward, ruffling his hands through his hair in agitation, "Mr Holmes, can this be true? Why? Why would a man whose son is about to marry my daughter want to kill my wife?"

Lestrade, his eyes wide like a fish which is flapping about hopelessly in the angler's net, pointed at Mr Doyle, "Constable Kingsley, take hold of Mr Doyle's wheelchair, we don't want him leaving us!" P.C. Kingsley did as he was bidden, and Lestrade held out his hands to Holmes in utter confusion, "Now, Holmes, *please*, explain this to me!"

"Certainly, Chief Inspector. Look at the evidence, Seumas Doyle, politician, naturalist, alpinist, mountaineer and explorer all over Europe and America, yet he makes a schoolboy error in saying there are grizzly bears in Canada, when he of all people would know perfectly well they are black bears! Secondly, why have we never heard of this great man's accident, surely such a loss to science and sport deserves sympathy for his plight? Why? Because the real Seumas Doyle is dead! Professor Rackham put us right on that score. The information returned to me via Wiggins that Doyle was buried at Glasnevin Cemetery in Dublin in 1908. In fact, Mr Doyle had retired to London since 1900 and it was at his son's insistence that his father's body be returned to their native Ireland. His son, *Ciaran* Doyle. There is no James Doyle…"

The young man, silent until now, gasped in horror, backing away from his father's wheelchair, "What? Are you saying I do not exist? Mr Holmes, what mean you? This man is my father is he not? And my mother, Helena, was she not his wife also?"

"My dear young man," Holmes began in a calming tone, "Yes, this man is your father, and of course, your mother was exactly whom you believed her to be. But this man lied about his true identity from the start, even to your mother. She was a nurse, you said, working in a sanatorium in Switzerland, near Meiringen? In the Interlaken District?" James nodded, "And you were born in 1892, yes?" James nodded again, his face pale with shock.

Holmes crouched before the wheelchair again, this time clutching the leather arm rests. It was then I saw his expression change, his eyes flash with anger, but only for a moment as he regained his composure. He spoke steadily and loudly, "You gave yourself away, sir, your own selfish wounded pride, the spider with his limbs pulled off! You talked bitterly of lying for hours until you were found, but you foolishly mentioned the waterfall…"

Old Doyle's eyes widened behind his spectacles; it was as if a mask had dropped away and I began to realise the import of the words Holmes spoke.

"I think you wanted me to know, didn't you?" he whispered then, the world no longer mattered, it was Holmes and his enemy. "You picked a very good identity to hide behind, but you never expected to have to raise your mask one more time! Did your men have the wit to tell you I had survived, or had I done my job well enough?"

Doyle clenched his fists, shaking them like a child who has been reprimanded for some minor offence. I had to see for myself and walked up to the man in the wheelchair and stared into his face, "Is it really, Holmes? You were so convinced he was dead!" I said, having only seen a photograph of the man in question printed in an academic monograph. I looked up at Constable Kingsley and as if to confirm it publicly, told him, "Constable, keep hold of that chair, the man sitting before you is none other than James Moriarty, the very Napoleon of crime himself!"

As soon as I uttered that fateful name the spell was finally broken, the villain was revealed for all to witness. He roared aloud, punching his fists into the arm rests of his chair. "Argh! Curse this chair and curse you Holmes! You pride yourself on your high moral stance, and yet you left me to die at the bottom of that waterfall! I cried out to you, begged for mercy, and yet you ignored me! I saw you looking down, how could you have failed to see or hear?" the creature howled. Surely he had forgotten that the roaring cataract would have carried his cries away on the wind, Holmes would never have known his enemy had survived. This I choose to believe; Sherlock Holmes would not leave any man to die, unless he was convinced it was the very Devil himself!

Doyle, now betrayed, continued, "Yes! Yes, I am Moriarty! But James, the apple of mine eye, you are my flesh and blood, my one true triumph! Out of the strong comes forth sweetness! A clever, honest boy who was going to aspire to the highest levels of the legal profession! What a delicious irony in my dotage, that Moriarty's son and heir should become a powerful lawyer! Yes, I told my beautiful nurse I was a mountaineer, and she accepted it. Perhaps staring death in the face softened my heart to womankind, but now I know it was only to her! Imagine my horror though, to find out the one woman my own child wishes to marry is the daughter of Irene Adler! I did not want my greatest final joke against the world to go that far!"

James looked as if he could vomit. Godfrey Norton looked at Moriarty, he was not angry, but heartbroken, "But how did Irene ever slight you? You were a myth, a bogieman to frighten young law students! I did not even believe that such a man as Moriarty existed! Why did you kill her?"

It seemed that even Moriarty had one ace left up his sleeve despite the inescapable position he now found himself in. He leered up at Godfrey, "You fool! I didn't intend to kill your wife! Oh no, it was her daughter! You don't know, *do you*?" He cackled and inclined his head towards Holmes.

I could not believe the gall of the man. But my friend was ready for him; he stood up and addressed Godfrey respectfully, "Mr Norton, my dear sir, I have to confess to you that your wife and I met up in Paris a few years after you were married. She wanted to see me, and I her. It was a whim, Irene thought it a marvellous joke, but despite our admiration for each other, that was as far as it went, a meeting of minds. She assured me her adventures were over, and that now she was expecting a child, her life was complete. Seeing me was merely to say a final farewell to that old life and ensure that I would not betray her. The dear lady wished me well and I did not see her again until this evening. I think my friend Moriarty imagined that the great detective let his guard down for the sake of Irene Adler... he imagined we had had an illicit affair which had produced a child... oh what twisted notions!" Holmes actually giggled. He turned back to Moriarty, "*You* wanted to kill Sophie because you thought she was *my* daughter! The son of James Moriarty marrying the daughter of Sherlock Holmes! That was a legacy you would never countenance, am I correct, Mr Moriarty?"

The latter buried his head in his hands, I could hear him making what I believed were anguished curses in his native tongue. But it would be to no avail, the spider was trapped in his own web of deceit. His child, now scarlet-faced with rage, edged past Holmes and pulled his father's hands away from his face, "Father? How could you have deceived us all? So my name is the same as the greatest villain in the

world? And you thought to destroy my happiness …
for what? A mistaken desire for revenge? Did you not
think it would kill me to know my own father would
countenance such a thing? I *love* Sophie! And now
your vengeance has only brought your house of cards
tumbling down upon your head, Mrs Norton is dead,
and you have destroyed this family. I shall henceforth
tell anyone who asks that both my parents are dead!"

"But my boy, my triumph, my Cuchulainn!"
Moriarty cried as James tore himself away from his
father's grasp and fled the auditorium.

Lestrade was beaming from ear to ear as if *he*
had made the great deduction, "Well, well, the great
Moriarty! Never did I think I'd see the day! You're
under arrest, sir, for the murder of Mrs Irene Norton,
and the attempted murder of Miss Sophie Norton!
Constable Kingsley, take Mr Moriarty away!" the
constable pushed the wheelchair up the central aisle to
cheers, whoops and hisses from the patrons who had
a grandstand view of the performance from the circle.
Lestrade turned to Mr Norton, "Mr Norton, I believe
I owe you an apology! Miss Norton is at the station

house along the road, we can call in on our way to Scotland Yard."

Without comment or apology to Holmes or me, Lestrade walked out with Mr Norton, leaving the three of us. "But Holmes," I started, "If Moriarty wanted to kill Sophie, why did he intend to use digitalis when it was her medicine? ... oh, of course, that I *should* know! If she were to be given too large a dose, she would also have cardiac arrest! Moriarty expected she would drink from the other glass and double up on that which she had already ingested! No-one would suspect it was murder, they would have just assumed that the medicine had proved ineffective! Yet he fell at the last hurdle when the housemaid presented the glass to Mrs Norton! What a villain, eh?" I looked at Mary sheepishly, realising she was near to tears after hearing of her young mistress's narrow escape.

Holmes nodded and smiled at me, "A villain to the last, my dear old friend!", and, ever the gentleman when the occasion truly merited, he turned to the little maid, "Mary, a thousand thank-yous for your courage, you observed correctly! Go and catch up with Lestrade, your young mistress will need your comfort more than ever now!" Mary smiled, wiping her eyes with her handkerchief, and ran off in the direction of the exit.

I let out a long sigh of relief. I looked at Holmes; he seemed drained at last, his eyes sunken a little, the lines of age showing a little more prominently than I had noticed earlier in the evening. The loss of such a significant person as *The Woman*, I believe, was going to leave its mark on my old friend. I patted his shoulder, "Sherlock Holmes... did you really have affection for Irene Adler? And did you really meet her in Paris? I'm just so surprised, I mean, I know you talked of her with admiration, and then when you met in the dressing room this evening, I have never seen you so animated, I did wonder myself."

"Affection? Mm, perhaps, I do have a heart of flesh, dear Watson, despite how you have portrayed me in your reports of our adventures, as the cold, reasoning machine! Admiration, certainly!" He paused, as if searching for appropriate words, "Irene Adler was the only woman who …might have elicited that most delicate, yet dangerous of emotions from me."

I had never heard him talk so honestly about her. But then, the logical reason flooded back as if this was a temporary slip, such as a music student may make in a recital, yet continues as if nothing is amiss. He pointed a finger to the sky, "But love merely blinds me to my true objectives! Did you not see tonight that I had to call upon the observational powers of others to shore up my deductions? I was distracted, distracted by the thought of seeing the lady performing on stage! No, Watson, I could never have married! But I did go to see her, Mrs Norton as she was by then, on her own request, and indeed, it would not take a detective to see she was already an expectant mother!"

I almost wanted him to confess that she had been his secret grand passion, but it seemed his role was ever to be the abstract reasoner, "I'm sorry all the same, I can see she did mean a lot to you." We walked up the centre aisle, Holmes retrieving his jacket and coat from the last row of the stalls where he had apparently left it earlier. The image of him cradling Mrs Norton in his arms suddenly flitted through my mind's eye again.

"By the way, Holmes, what *did* you say to Irene? I recall her words to you distinctly, '*No, she is not, would that she had been!*'" I asked, a sense of dread creeping into my heart.

"I asked a ridiculously improbable question, despite having the information already... I asked her if Sophie was our child," Holmes said guilelessly without meeting my gaze.

I was aghast, "But you already said she was expecting the baby when you met her..." I do not flatter myself that I possess Holmes' great observational powers, but I know when a man is obfuscating, "Are you... *lying* to me, Holmes? After all this time...?"

Sherlock Holmes grinned secretively and turned to me, his grey eyes twinkling. "I should have thought the answer to that question, my dear Watson, is ...elementary!"

THE END

Historical Note:

The character of 'Seumas Doyle' is a mash-up of many historical figures that existed within the lifetimes of Sherlock Holmes and John Watson. Of course, he was a convenient character for Holmes' nemesis, Moriarty to adopt. The Irish mountaineer's story ensured Moriarty had explanations for everything from his marriage to a Swiss nurse to his disability.

The Alpine Club was indeed founded in 1857, but by English mountaineer, William Matthews. The Palliser Expedition took place 1857-60 led by geographer, John Palliser, an Englishman. James Hector, a Scots naturalist, was a member of the team which accompanied Palliser. Henry Bruen the Younger was the M.P. for Carlow County in the UK Government 1857-1880. Bruen was also a J.P. and High Sheriff of both Carlow and Wexford. The 'real' Seamus Doyle was a twentieth century Sinn Féin member and politician; he, like many nationalists of his time, was opposed to the Anglo-Irish Treaty of 1921. Of course, using the name Doyle was my deliberate choice.

My story, as was the case with Conan Doyle's work, is entirely **FICTIONAL**, but I have attempted to meld historical detail with Conan Doyle's traditional world of Holmes and Watson.

Also from Fiona Jane Brown

"Dr Brown has written another play, "Sherlock Holmes & the Adventure of the Jacobite Rose", a clever and entertaining drama, ideal for youth groups and schools.

Sherlock Holmes Society of London

"The deductions from Holmes are logical and sound. Humour plays an important part too and the script has many moments which made me smile for all the right reasons. Well-researched, well thought out and well plotted. A delight to read and one would think a joy to perform also."

The Baker Street Society

www.ingramcontent.com/pod-product-compliance
Lightning Source LLC
Chambersburg PA
CBHW071335130626
46556CB00004B/1914

®

Beyond the Darkness

My feelings are on the outside.

While the outside is on the inside.

What should be covered is now exposed.

I'm in balls and knots, can you help me?

Help me cover the inside?

It hurts.

From the fact of me being hurt.

My insides die slowly.

I'm still hurting.

Through all of the hurt;

I forgive you.

- ■ Susan M. Smith